D0575495

The
Frog
in
the
Well

The Frog in the Well

by Alvin Tresselt
illustrated by
Roger Duvoisin

Chadron State College Library
Chadron, Nebraska

OTHROP, LEE & SHEPARD CO., INC. · NEW YORK

©, 1958 by Alvin Tresselt and Roger Duvoisin
Library of Congress Catalog Card Number: 58-11819

ted in the U.S.A.   Seventh printing, October, 1966   All rights reserved

There was once a frog who lived in a well,
and a fine well it was, too.
It was cool and deep, with mossy rocks.
Just right for a cool green frog.
The bottom was a pool of clear cool water.
Just right for swimming and splashing—
Just right for telling this little frog what a handsome
frog he was!
The top of the well was a ceiling of blue sky,
with fluffy clouds passing.

Sometimes at night the moon looked down the well
to wink at this happy frog on his bed of moss.
And what with all the foolish flies and bugs that were
curious as to what might be at the bottom of a well,
there was plenty for a little green frog to eat.

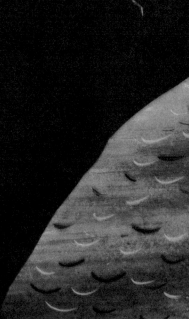

Now since this frog had lived in his well for longer than
he could remember, he had one very strange idea.
He thought his well was the whole world!
He didn't know what a daisy looked like.
Or what a spring day smelled like.
He had never sat on a log and croaked all night.
He had never sunned himself on a lily pad.
He didn't even know another frog!
"The world is nothing but moss-covered rocks," he said,
"with a pool of water at the bottom."
But then came a day when all the water
disappeared from the well and no more curious bugs
came down to see what a well looked like.

Now what was this foolish frog to do?
No water to swim in.
No mirror to tell him what a handsome frog he was.
No bugs to eat!

"I had better see what is at the end of the world," grumbled the frog, "while I still have the strength to hop."

He flipped out his tongue to catch the first curious bug he had seen in days, and then started hopping up to the top of the well.

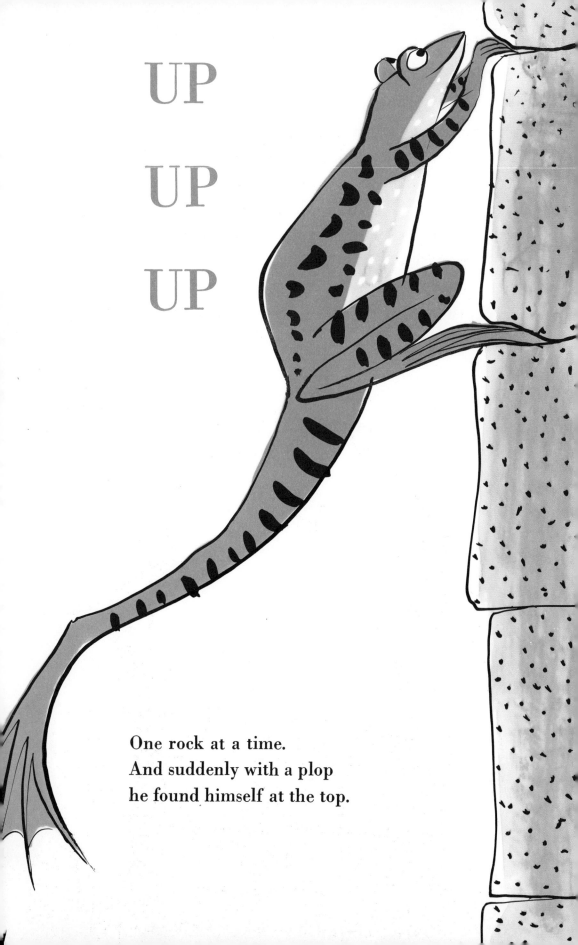

UP

UP

UP

One rock at a time.
And suddenly with a plop
he found himself at the top.

But what was this?
Trees blowing in a blowy wind.
Sunshine on his shiny green back.
And a clump of daisies, all white and yellow!
The little frog was so surprised
that he just sat and blinked.
But at that moment a most attractive bug
lighted on a daisy face.
"That's better," he said as he finished off the bug.
"And now that I have come to the end of the world
I think I'll look around a bit."

Off he went through the meadow grass,
stopping only to eat every once in a while.
He presently arrived at the muddy bank of a stream,
but he had no sooner jumped in for a swim when he
heard a low Moooooo, right over his head!

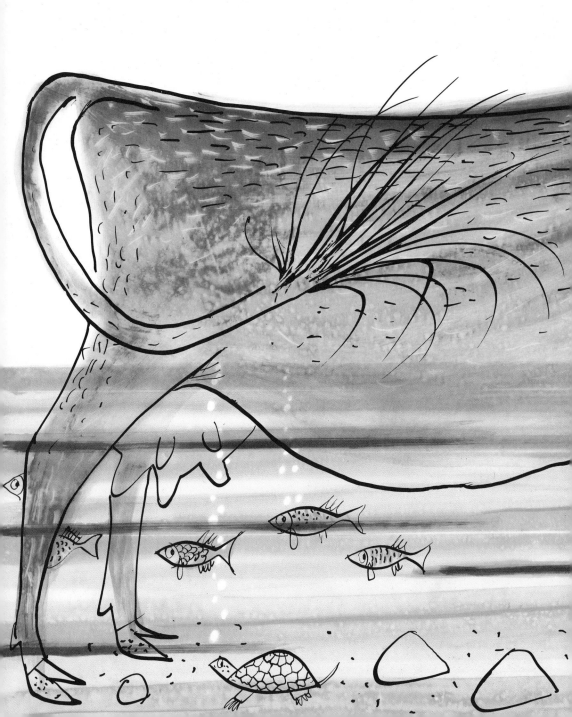

"Are you an end-of-the-world creature?" asked the frog,
sounding much braver than he felt.
"Heavens no, I'm a cow," said the cow.
"And this isn't the end of the world—it *is* the world.
It's my pasture. The world ends over there on the other
side of the barn."
And with that she busied herself
with a long drink of water.
Hopping nimbly out of the way, the little green frog
decided to follow the stream, through the grassy
meadow and into a marsh.

But then what a chattering and squeaking he heard!
With dozens of blackbirds)bobbing and
swaying on the tall rushes.
"Are *you* an end-of-the-world creature?" asked the frog
as one of the birds rested for a minute nearby.
"I'm a bird," skreaked the bird. "And the world
doesn't end until you reach the edge of the land.
It's a long way away though, because I have never
reached it, so I don't worry about it.
Besides," said the bird as he fluttered away, "this
much of the world is quite big enough for me."

The green frog was very puzzled by now.
"There is more to the world than my well," said he,
for he was now beginning to grow wise.
"I will follow the brook and see what there is to see."
Through the marsh and into the woods went the
brook, and with a hop and a plop, through the marsh
and into the woods went the frog.

Chadron State College Library
Chadron, Nebraska

Here in the cool shadows, where the brook talked
quietly to the pebbles as it bubbled along, the green frog
met animals of the woodland world—the deer and the
fox, the squirrel and the bear.
And they all told him that theirs was a very fine world,
here in the woods.

"The world outside my world grows more and more interesting," said the frog as he stopped for lunch on a rock.

"But I will follow the brook until it ends, and I will see what I will see."

He didn't have far to go before the brook slipped quietly into a lake, just as soft drops of rain came pattering down through the leaves of the trees.

This was something a frog that had lived all his life in a well had never known about.

Splish, splash—and the raindrops falling on his back felt so good that the little green frog just swelled up his throat and began to sing—chug-a-rum, chug-a-rum, chug-a-rum.

Then he stopped a minute to catch his breath, and what
did he hear?
Frogs! Millions of frogs!
Garumphing and croaking and chug-a-rumming
in the rain.

The little frog sat there a minute thinking.
He thought of the cow and her world in the pasture.
He thought of the bird and his world in the marsh.
He thought of the forest animals
in their woodland world.
And he thought of his little green frog world in the well.
"Now that there is water falling out of the sky," he
thought, "the well may fill up again. Perhaps I had
better go back to my little world of mossy rocks
once more."
But then he listened again to the beautiful music
of a million frogs.
And the frog, who by now had grown
very wise indeed, said,

"A foolish frog *can* be happy all alone at the bottom of
a well, but a clever frog can be much happier out here."
And with that he sprang up into the air
with his long strong legs.
It was the longest leap he had ever made, and he landed

—plop—right in the middle of the million singing frogs!